A WILDERNESS PASSOVER

"Let all who are hungry come and eat."
The Passover Haggadah (guidebook for the seder meal)

To Mrs. Bess Laderman and my parents, Harold and Lee Cook
and in memory of Rabbi Manuel Laderman
and my grandparents, Louis and Susie Cook

K.C.W.

To my husband, Terry, for his vision and belief in me,
and to my daughter, Elisha, for her loving support.

L.G.

Text copyright © 1994 Kathleen Cook Waldron
Illustration copyright © 1994 Leslie Gould

Northern Lights Books for Children are published by
Red Deer College Press
56 Avenue & 32 Street Box 5005
Red Deer Alberta Canada T4N 5H5

Acknowledgements
Edited for the Press by Tim Wynne-Jones
Designed by Christine Toller
Printed in Korea
for Red Deer College Press

The Alberta
Foundation
for the Arts

Providing a foundation for the arts

ALBERTA
Lotteries
THE SOURCE
OF MANY BENEFITS

Financial support provided by the Alberta Foundation for
the Arts, a beneficiary of the Lottery Fund of the
Government of Alberta, and by the Canada Council, the
Department of Communications and Red Deer College.

Canadian Cataloguing in Publication Data

Waldron, Kathleen Cook.
A wilderness passover

(Northern lights books for children)
ISBN 0-88995-112-8

1. Passover—Juvenile literature.   I. Gould, Leslie, 1949
II. Title.   III. Series.   PS8595.A549W5 1994
jC813'.54   C93-091920-3   PZ7.W437Wi 1994

A WILDERNESS PASSOVER

written by Kathleen Cook Waldron

illustrated by Leslie Gould

NORTHERN LIGHTS BOOKS FOR CHILDREN

LAST night Louie led the search with a candle. Susan followed with a goose feather and Papa with a wooden spoon and a bag. They were searching for any bread, cake, cookie or cracker crumbs left in the house.

The kitchen glistened in the candlelight as Susan swept the last crumbs into Papa's wooden spoon. After their first winter in the mountains at Ruby Lake, Louie's family was finally ready for Passover.

Or so it seemed.

The morning sun stretched through the new green leaves and danced on the creek below. Papa, Louie and Susan stood outside by a little fire burning the crumbs. Mama sat in Grandpa's old chair on the porch and frowned.

"Mama and I will do your chores today," Papa said, "while you two pick up the eggs and shankbone for the seder tonight."

"Great," said Susan.

"Sure," said Louie.

"No!" said Mama.

"WHAT?" asked Papa, Susan and Louie.

"No seder," Mama repeated. "How can you even consider having a seder here in the middle of nowhere?"

"Why not?" asked Louie.

"Ppph! We have no matzah, no parsley, no horseradish, no haroset, no special wine. Nothing!"

"We have flour and water," Papa said. "We could bake our own matzah. Like our ancestors did in Egypt."

Susan pulled up a fistful of green grass and placed it in Mama's lap. "Who needs parsley?" she said. "We're surrounded by spring greens."

Louie ran across the yard, broke off a willow branch and peeled off some bark. He gave the branch to Mama. "I bet bark's a better bitter herb than horseradish," he said. "Rabbits and deer eat it." He took a small bite and quickly spit it out. "Yuck! Now that's bitter!"

Mama handed the branch back to Louie and brushed the grass off her lap. "We are not rabbits or deer. Or cows."

Susan picked up a shovel and started digging. "How about a dandelion root for the bitter herb?" she asked, shaking the dirt off an enormous dandelion. "And dandelion leaves can be our spring green."

"Dandelions?" Mama rocked harder in her chair. "What about the wine? How can we have a seder without special wine?"

"Let's use the wild raspberry juice we canned last summer," Louie said. "Elijah might like juice for a change."

"I'd much rather drink four glasses of raspberry juice than four glasses of watered-down wine," said Susan.

"And the haroset?" Mama asked, daring them to answer. Every year she made a huge bowl of haroset, the sweet apple reminder of the mortar the slaves once made. "The few shriveled apples we have wouldn't make enough mortar to stick two bricks together, much less build two cities."

"We'll make do," Papa replied.

Mama shook her head. "Even if we bake our own matzah, pick dandelions, drink raspberry juice and share a splotch of haroset, how can we have a seder with just four people?"

No one answered.

Everyone knew Mama's real complaint wasn't with the food. Mama missed preparing for Passover with her aunties, uncles, cousins and friends. She missed greeting all the guests that Grandpa invited to their seders. "No one should be alone at Passover," Grandpa had always said.

"Look on the bright side, Mama," said Susan. "Louie won't be afraid to ask the Four Questions if only four of us are at the seder."

"I wasn't afraid last year," Louie argued. "I just forgot the first question."

"Enough," said Papa. "We have a lot of work to do before sunset."

"I give up," said Mama. She closed her eyes and leaned back in her chair. Louie ran to get his bike. Papa headed for the woodshed.

Susan carried the dandelion into the house, but on her way to the kitchen she stopped. A picture drew her over to the mantel—the baby picture of her sitting on Grandpa's lap at a long-ago seder. Mama misses him most of all, she realized. Tonight will be her first seder without him, her first Passover away from her family in the city—a Passover in the wilderness.

Then Susan had an idea. She dropped the dandelion in the sink, took a seder book off the shelf, tucked it in her sweater pocket and ran back outside.

She jumped on her bike and sprinted down the driveway after Louie. "I have a plan!" she said breathlessly as she caught up with him. They turned onto the main road and raced to Millie's farm.

After a quick cup of tea with Millie, they packed the eggs safely into Louie's backpack and headed for their next stop—the Higgins' ranch. On the way they passed the Cugnets, who were out working in their orchard.

At Higgins' ranch the whole family was outside helping
Stan, the sheep shearer, with the shearing. Mrs. Higgins was
glad to stop for a bit and bring them the shankbone.

On the way home, Susan and Louie saw Mr. Morgan walking along the road with his fishing pole. He lived alone and never visited the other neighbors. Louie raced up the hill to him. "Hey, Mr. Morgan!" he called.

Louie walked his bike alongside Mr. Morgan and chatted away. Susan hung back. She had never spoken to him before.

At home Susan put the eggs on to boil while Louie mixed salt water. Papa had lit the wood stove and was busy baking matzah. A pot of chicken soup bubbled on the stove. Racks of macaroons cooled on the windowsill. Susan roasted the shankbone and an egg for the seder plate. All afternoon Papa, Louie and Susan peeled and chopped, sliced, simmered, steamed and baked.

Mama sat outside, polishing Elijah's cup.

Shortly before sunset, Susan opened the table to its fullest size and covered it with their best linen cloth. Even with just four places set, the table reminded Susan of Grandpa's.

At sunset Mama came inside to light the festival candles with Susan. They were about to sit down when they heard a loud knocking at the door.

"Isn't Elijah a little early tonight?" Papa asked.

"Since when does Elijah knock?" asked Mama.

Papa opened the door, and then he opened his mouth, but no words came out. A crowd of neighbors greeted him from the porch.

"Come in," he said at last. "Welcome to our seder."

Millie came in first with a basket of wild strawberries and a big bouquet of daffodils from her garden.

Mr. Higgins followed with a huge horseradish root he'd dug that morning. "Plant a small piece," he advised, "and you'll have plenty by fall."

Mrs. Higgins brought fresh parsley from her garden. Her son Danny had a jar of pickles in each hand. His sister Patty was carrying an overflowing green salad. Stan followed with a steaming dish of asparagus.

Mrs. Cugnet was next with a big bowl of haroset. "Susan gave me the recipe," she said, "and I had plenty of apples left from last year's harvest."

"Will apple wine be all right?" Mr. Cugnet asked. "It's my own special recipe."

Mama's eyes shone like the festival candles.

Susan and Louie set more places at the table. The wine cups were filled and the seder began.

When the time came for Louie to ask the Four Questions, there was a soft knocking on the door.

"Elijah?" Mama asked. Susan and Louie exchanged glances.

Papa opened the door. "It's Mr. Morgan," he said.

Mr. Morgan held out a platter of fish. "Is trout allowed?" he asked shyly.

"Trout is perfect," Mama replied. And she set another place at the table.

"Louie," Papa asked, "are you ready to ask the Four Questions?"

Louie picked up his seder book, looked around the table, took a deep breath and in his clearest voice sang out:

"Why is this night different from all other nights?"

Why *is* this night different from all other nights?

Passover is a joyful Jewish holiday celebrating freedom and the arrival of spring. It is a time to recall the past, celebrate the present and express hope for the future. As we remember how many thousands of Hebrew slaves left Egypt and miraculously crossed the Red Sea on dry land, received the Ten Commandments at Mount Sinai, survived in the wilderness for forty years then began a new life in freedom in the Promised Land, we renew our hope that one day all people may be free.

Preparing for Passover includes a complete spring cleaning, especially in the kitchen. The night before Passover begins, the house is searched for any hidden crumbs of food with leavening. The following morning, the crumbs are burned in a small fire outside. In place of regular bread, only unleavened bread, or matzah (*mat*-zuh), may be eaten during the eight days of Passover as a reminder of how quickly the slaves had to escape from Egypt. They didn't even have time to let their bread rise.

Like all Jewish holidays, Passover begins at sunset with the lighting of the festival candles. Families then sit down with friends and guests for a ritual seder (*say*-dur) meal—a feast of traditional foods, songs, prayers, historical stories and games in which everyone participates.

"Why is this night different from all other nights?" the youngest child asks at the beginning of the seder. Why do we eat matzah and bitter herbs? Why do we dip two different foods and sit a certain way at the table?

The answers to these questions recount the exodus from slavery to freedom. Traditional foods found on every seder table help to tell the story:

Wine is served for celebration, enough for four cups for everyone present, two before dinner and two after. A special cup is set for the prophet Elijah, the messenger of peace and helper of the needy, who represents the stranger always to be welcomed at the table. After dinner, the door is opened for Elijah to come in and drink his wine.

A fresh green represents springtime, the renewal of life.

Salt water is a reminder of the slaves' tears.

A shankbone symbolizes sacrifice.

Matzah, the unleavened bread, is the central symbol of Passover.

A bitter herb symbolizes the bitterness of slavery.

Haroset (hah-*roe*-set) is a delicious mixture of finely chopped apples, nuts, cinnamon and wine, symbolizing the mortar used to build the cities of Pithom and Ramses.

A roasted boiled egg represents both sacrifice and the cycle of life.

Setting the seder table also includes **Haggadahs** (hah-*gah*-dohs), books with the seder service for everyone to follow, plus **a cushion or pillow** for the leader of the seder to relax in comfort, a sign of freedom.

In preserving the ancient Passover traditions, families maintain a strong sense of historic and spiritual unity. At the same time, each family is free to add its own special traditions, making every seder truly unique.